Someone Like You

Epiphany Hightower

Fulton Books
Meadville, PA

Published by Fulton Books 2023

ISBN 979-8-88982-681-1 (paperback)
ISBN 979-8-88982-683-5 (digital)

Printed in the United States of America

CHAPTER 1

Kennedi

"Surprise!" I heard as my new fiancé, Derrick, and I walked into my mom's house for Sunday dinner.

"Wow! Thank you, all!" I said as my mom went to give Derrick a hug.

"I'm so glad you are going to be a part of this family," she said.

"Well, I am glad Kennedi finally said yes this time," Derrick said, looking at me with his light-brown eyes while my mom dragged him away to mingle with people at this surprise engagement party.

Derrick and I met six years ago when we were both working in the same building as lawyers. Since I am a contract lawyer and Derrick is a prosecutor's attorney, that is how we met. He was not the usual type I would go for, but dating my usual type has not gotten me anywhere close to the altar. I just turned thirty years old, and my biological clock is ticking. Derrick is a good guy, comes from a great family, and has a great career that is only getting better from here. I may not be totally in love with him, but marriage does not always need love. My marriage will be built on financial and career stability so that I will be able to live with it for the rest of my life. As I look around the large living room filled with mostly my mom's friends and some of Derrick's and my colleagues, I cannot help but have doubts about everything that I just said.

CHAPTER 2
Julian

"J, you are working the twelve-hour shift today?" I heard Thomas ask as I was walking into Caves Tow Trucking Company, getting ready to get into one of the trucks.

"Yeah, I have to make this extra since I missed a day of work to take G-ma to the doctor," I replied.

Thank God I lived right next door to her and was stopping by anyway to spend time with her, because I don't know what I could have done without her.

"I hope she feels better," Thomas said, referring to my grandmother, who has raised me since the age of five, when both of my parents died in a car crash.

She has been there for me ever since. Now I'm twenty-five years old and trying to save up for my own trucking company. So my main focus is on my grandmother and stacking money. I do have a few fuck buddies from time to time when I am in the mood, but other than that, I have never met a woman with whom I wanted more. So until then, I will be single and doing me, and that now requires me to be on the road for twelve hours.

CHAPTER 3
Kennedi

Me and Derrick do not live together by choice, so I woke up this morning and got a text from Derrick saying, "We must go to a black-and-white gala today. Be ready by seven thirty." *I love you too,* I said to myself as I was already getting ready to have lunch with my friend Gabriella. I guess I will have to drag her with me to go looking for a dress for the gala tonight.

"Hey, girl," I said to Gabriella as I approached the table.

Gabriella is what I would call a knockout plus-size beauty, and she rocks it very well. She has worked with me as a paralegal for about three years, and she has been a great friend to me ever since.

"Hey, Kennedi. I just ordered a drink for you, boo."

"Thanks," I said.

"You are looking cute as usual."

"Thanks, so do you."

I felt cute with my short bob, freshly blown out, and I went and had a spa day to get ready for the gala tonight.

"I haven't seen you since you got engaged," she said.

"Yeah, I have been super busy getting everything in order, you know. Derrick wants a big elaborate weeding to show off to his colleagues, and you know my mother is all excited about the wedding to show off to all her friends," I said.

"But are you happy about actually being married to Derrick for the rest of your life? Do you really love him? And you always complain that he does not satisfy you sexually, and you are willing to spend your whole life with him."

No.

"Well, I have a vibrator, and who really marries for love anyway? Marriage is about financial stability and future career success, and then love should come."

"You know what? I'm going to pretend that I didn't hear what you said and give you some advice that my dad gives me when it comes to relationships:

'Love is like shores. Sometimes it seems like you are riding such a high wave, and then the next moment, it seems like the waves are steady, but if you are loving the right person, the lows will never get too low and the highs will have you feeling so blessed that two souls that were once lost were found with each other.'"

I did not even have a response to what she just said. I just sat there and twirled my ring around, pondering if I could go through with marrying Derrick.

CHAPTER 4
Julian

Damn, it is really raining hard out here, and I am on the eighth hour of my twelve-hour shift. I was going through a call about picking up an abandoned car that was in a parking lot when I spotted a car on the side of the road with the taillights on, so I could not keep going without checking out who was in the car stranded. I stepped out of the car. It seemed like as soon as I stepped out of my truck, I approached the car and knocked on the window to see who was in it.

"Excuse me. I work for a car towing company. I can get your car for you if you like," I said.

The person in the car rolled down the window a little bit, and I heard the sweetest voice I have ever heard.

"I am trying to get in touch with my fiancée, who should pick up the phone any minute," she said.

"Well, how about I wait for about ten minutes, and if you cannot get in contact with anyone, then I can take you to where you need to go," I said.

"Well, that is very nice of you, but my fiancée should answer shortly," she said.

I started walking back to the truck to get in and wait just in case her punk-ass fiancée did not answer the phone. When you see your woman calling you multiple times, not answering the phone is very suspicious. Not even five minutes later, I saw my passenger side door being opened, and I saw the most beautiful and angelic face soaked in the rain. When I traveled south, her ruby-red lips looked perfect against her beautiful cinnamon-brown complexion, and the dress she had on was making it very difficult not to ogle at her exposed cleavage.

"Excuse me. Can you help me with the truck?"

She brought me back from dreaming as she stretched her hand out to me. When I went to lean over and grab her hand to help her in the truck. I got a sniff of her perfume, which started to make things pretty hard. *Why is she having this effect on me? Maybe I am horny. I have not had sex in about a month. Maybe it is time for me to call one of my friends to handle this situation*, I thought to myself as I looked at her through my peripheral vision, got situated into the seat, and sat down wearing the black dress that had slits on the side that showed off her nice thighs. I had to bite my lip to keep from moaning out loud. Well, this is going to be a long ride.

CHAPTER 5
Kennedi

As I sat next to this very sexy stranger, I had to do my best to discreetly look him over, with his chocolate skin and his dreads neatly done as they stopped at his shoulder. I looked over at his hands gripping the steering wheel, which made me think of him gripping my…

"So where do you need to go?" I heard him ask.

"Well, I was supposed to be at this gala supporting my fiancée, but it is almost over, so you could go and take me home. We are heading in the right direction, just three more blocks and a left turn," I said.

"So the reason your man could not answer his phone when he sees his fiancé calling is because he is busy entertaining people at a party?" he said.

"Well, first of all, it is not just some party. My fiancée is an attorney, and he is up for the next prosecuting attorney position and has to mingle with other attorneys and senators, and the music was probably loud and…," she said.

"So, if you want to excuse your fiancée's behavior over some loud music and why he could not answer, then that is your business."

"Yes, it is my business. I don't even know why I'm explaining myself to you anyway. I don't see a ring on your finger, and I'm pretty sure you are not in a serious relationship. You don't know me, so you cannot tell me anything about *my* relationship!" I said, fuming.

He said nothing else to me the rest of the way. A few minutes later, I noticed the truck coming to a stop, and the rain had calmed down slightly. It was just 10:00 p.m. night sky, and we were coming to a complete stop right in front of my house.

I started to take off my seat belt, and in a dismissive tone, I said, "Thanks for the ride."

"Look," I heard him say.

"This is the card to a mechanic who happens to be a friend of mine. You call him, and he will pick your car up and take it to his shop to get it fixed."

"Thanks," I said.

I noticed that he stayed until I made it safely inside. I walked inside my home and shut the door in a frustrated manner. I could not believe I had let a stranger tell me about my own relationship. Then why do I want to fuck this sexy stranger so badly?

CHAPTER 6
Julian

"Fuck! Julian, I am about to cum, Daddy!" she said.

"Shit! You better hurry up!" I said, about to empty out this condom.

"I'm cumming."

When I got home from work, I had to call up one of my friends to help take care of the problem of the slick-mouthed, sexy passenger I never got the name of, but I can't get her out of my head. I never had a problem where I wanted a woman as badly as I wanted her. Maybe it is the fact that I cannot have her.

"So, I was thinking that we should go on an official date?" the girl asked.

"Look, I don't even remember your name, and you knew exactly what it was. So now this is just a fuck session, and it is over. You can go home now," I said.

"Fuck you, Julian! And my name is Jasmine, asshole!" she said as she got up out of bed and started putting on her clothes as she headed toward the door.

"Thomas, man, did a girl call and ask you about having her car towed?" I asked.

It was officially Monday, and I could not wait to see if she had called so she could get her car taken care of.

"Yeah, a Kennedi called me and said she got my card from a guy, and when she explained, I knew exactly who she was talking about," Thomas said.

"Ahh, so her name is Kennedi. Interesting," I said.

Thomas turned around and looked at me in an interesting way.

"What is that look about, bro? I know she is bad as hell, but she is engaged, and we have to respect that."

We both stopped, looked at each other, and burst out laughing.

"When has that ever stopped us from taking a Niggas woman?" I said.

"Yeah, you're right, but you may not ever see her again. It's not like we all run in the same circles," Thomas said.

CHAPTER 7
Kennedi

"Gabriella, can you get me the paperwork on the new property?" I said over the intercom to Gabriella's office.

"Be there in five minutes," she said.

While I was waiting on her, there was a knock on my door from Derrick. We have not been getting along since that incident over the weekend where I was stranded. He never picked up his phone and blamed me for not showing up at the gala to look good by his side for appearances.

"Would you like to have lunch today?" he asked.

He looked good in his button-up shirt and gray slacks.

"Sorry, but I have to work through lunch today. I'm so glad it's Friday, and me and Gabriella are going to have our annual girls' night in tonight."

"Yeah, speaking of girl's night in, I hope you guys will be looking at wedding pictures, and we still have to pick a wedding date," Derrick said.

"I…"

Before I was able to respond, Gabriella walked into my office, looking at me and Derrick.

"Sorry. It took me a while to bring these files," Gabriella said.

"No problem," I said.

Before walking out, she gave me a look, saying we were going to talk about why the tension in the room was so thick between my fiancée and me.

"We have only been engaged for a month, and I feel we should wait awhile before we make any date for our wedding," I said.

"Well, I would like to get married this year if it is possible. Nothing big. Just me, you, your mother, my parents, and a few close friends are all we need to have at the wedding."

"Well, I have a lot of work to do before the weekend, so we can finish this conversation on Sunday when I am finished with my at-home girl-friend getaway."

"Also, speaking of home, you should be working on getting ready to come live with me when we get married."

I looked at him like he had lost his mind.

"Why can't you come and live with me?" I asked.

"That is not how it works. You are supposed to come live with me," he said.

I could not believe what I was hearing.

"You know what? I don't even know who I'm talking to. I think you need to go, and we can talk later."

I focused on my computer and did not even notice when he walked out of my office.

CHAPTER 8
Julian

"J, let's stop over at this store. I have the munchies," Thomas said.

Today is Friday. Thomas and I work together for twelve hours, and we usually load up on snacks at the local grocery store. We walked into the store, and I noticed two women.

Because their asses were both turned back to me, I enjoyed the view nicely until I heard Thomas say, "Gabriella, is that you?"

Both of the women turned around, and the taller of the two looked like she was trying to figure out how she knew Thomas.

Then it registered on her face as she said, "Thomas, I haven't seen you since high school. How are you?"

While they were talking, I noticed that the girl she was with was the same girl I picked up that night. She was dressed down in some leggings and an over-size white T-shirt. I have never seen someone dress as sexy as she did.

"This is Julian, my friend and work partner," Thomas said to Gabriella.

"You two already know each other?" Thomas said, pointing to me and Kennedi.

"Well, not officially. Hi, I'm Julian," I said as I stuck my hand out for her to shake.

"Hello, I'm Kennedi," she said as we both stared each other in the eyes.

"Me and Kennedi work together at a law office. She is a contract lawyer, and I have been her paralegal for three years. We have been friends ever since."

Gabriella jumped in, breaking up the sexual tension happening between me and Kennedi.

"Well, it was good seeing you, Gabriella. You have my contact information, and I hope to see you both on Sunday," Thomas said, and we just turned and walked away, but not without me stealing one last glance at Kennedi.

CHAPTER 9
Kennedi

We finally left the grocery store after bumping into the man that sex dreams are made of. Gabriella and I always go to the store to pile up on junk food to get ready for our girls' night in, and the last thing I expected to see was the man who helped me with my car, who knew Gabriella, and his friend, whom I was not able to get out of my mind for the past few weeks. Seeing him in person after all those weeks, I realized how fine he is.

"Didn't Thomas look so good? I have not seen him since my high school graduation," Gabriella said.

This took me out of those thoughts about another man that I should not be having, considering I am engaged.

"Do not think I did not notice the way you and Julian were looking at each other back there," Gabriella said.

"We were not looking at each other in any particular way," I said, trying to convince myself that the only reason I am feeling this way is because Derrick and I have not had sex in a few weeks, even though whenever we do have sex, I can count on one hand how many times he has made me cum.

"Uh, umm, well, do you plan on coming with me to their poetry reading on Sunday?" Gabriella asked.

"I don't know if I should, and besides, I—"

"Know you have to come with me to be my wingwoman against the inner hoe in me that wants to come out when I look at Thomas."

We both looked at each other seriously, and then we busted out laughing.

"Girl, you are so crazy! I will see. Maybe I will bring Derrick with me," I said, knowing I should put on my poker face when I see Julian.

CHAPTER 10

Julian

It is finally Saturday morning, and I walked over to the house on the right to visit my G-ma. When the opportunity came to live right next door to my grandmother, I took it.

"Good morning, G-ma," I said, making my way into the kitchen where she was cooking breakfast—pancakes, sausage, bacon, potatoes, and grits.

"Good morning, baby. How was your night?"

"It was good."

"Yeah, I saw that young lady walking into your house late last night. Is she coming by anytime to meet me?"

"G-ma, there is no special woman in my life that you have to worry about meeting anytime soon. I just have female friends who don't mind keeping me company every now and then," I said as I thought about Kennedi, the woman to whom I barely said five words, and I wondered if her soon-to-be husband appreciated all that comes with her.

"Well, if you would read your beautiful poetry a lot more, then you would have no problem finding a wife. I want you to experience the true unconditional love that your grandfather and I experienced for forty years before God called him home."

"I know how much you loved each other. Hopefully, one day, I will experience that type of love."

"You are the best grandson a woman can ask for and want."

CHAPTER 11
Kennedi

"Good morning," Derek said.

It was 7:00 a.m. on a Sunday. Gabriella went back to her house late Saturday night. I knew that Derek was coming over to have sex because it had not happened in a couple of weeks. I'm not complaining, though, because my vibrator makes me cum more than he does. But he thinks he is pleasing my body, but all he is doing is focusing on pleasing himself and his own pleasure. To be honest, our sex life is like our relationship. The only reason we are really in this relationship is because it can both help us excel in our careers in law. I am a contract lawyer, so the more people I get, the higher my profile will get in the business, and I can start my own firm. I believe everyone gets married for one reason or another, and mine happens to be about career climbing.

"Hi, Derek," I said as I noticed him looking at my body seductively.

I was wearing shorts and a tank top with no bra on, and my breasts and ass were spilling out of my shorts and top.

"Are you still mad at me?" he asked as we walked back to my bedroom.

"No, not really," I said as he walked up to me and started kissing me, his hands going into my pants and rubbing my clit.

"Are you always this wet for Daddy?" Derrick said, as he started to rub on my clit faster and faster.

"Um, yes, Daddy," I said as I was getting close to cumming.

"No, you can't come now. I want to make you cum with my dick," he said as he removed his hand.

"No, I was almost there," I said as he pushed me back on the bed.

"It's okay. I want to feel you cum on my dick," he said as he started to crawl on the bed with his pants already off, and I could see his dick on hard, 6-in-medium at best.

"Shit!" he hissed when he entered me, and five minutes later, he had already come, filling the condom.

"That was great!" he said.

I just lay there and could not believe that I did not cum.

"I have to go take a shower," I said as I walked to my bathroom, butt naked.

I turned on the water, planning to finish the job myself. I started rubbing on my clit, and the more I got going, the face I was fantasizing about was the man I keep running into in the most impromptu times, Julian, who made me cum the hardest.

CHAPTER 12
Julian

I was a little nervous when it came to me reading my poems in front of people, but writing poems has always been my way of escaping from the world and writing down exactly what is my driving force, and sometimes I say something off the dome. I started coming here when Thomas started playing the piano for different independent artists who come to the jazz club, and he convinced me to start reading my poems. I have gotten a lot of play from women while doing this. They seemed surprised when they saw a six-foot man with dreads come to the stage and tell a full story within five minutes, using only a few words to express what he was trying to say.

"It's a good crowd out there tonight," Thomas said as he finished playing on stage.

"Oh, really, that's good," I said.

"My girl is also out there with your girl," Thomas said, and I peeked out the curtain and saw the girl whom Thomas could not stop staring at when we ran into them at the store, and sitting beside her was the woman I could not get out of my mind since I saw her on the side of the road. Her face was lightly made up, and she was wearing red lipstick that made her lips look even more plump. When her lips parted, I could see her beautiful smile, and I noticed a man sitting next to her with one arm wrapped around her shoulders and the other one holding his phone.

"Alright, guys, our next opening act is a brotha who spills gold from his lips. Welcome to the stage, Julian!" the announcer said.

As soon as I walked to the stage, there were many women catcalling and snapping.

"Good evening, everyone. I have recently written this poem, and I hope you guys enjoy it.

"*Sweet Ways, is it her way that has me thinking that she could be the one that makes my spine quiver, make my heart speed. The look in her eyes tells me everything I need to know about her sweet ways…*"

While I was reading the poem, I kept eye contact with her the whole time, and I could see my words taking a toll on her. Once the showcase was over, I saw Thomas talking to the girl Gabriella and her friend Kennedi, smiling and talking as I walked over to where they were gathered.

Gabriella was the first person to say, "Great poem, Julian."

"Thanks," I said to Gabriella, then she focused all her attention back on Thomas.

"So what did you think of my poem?" I asked Kennedi since she was standing directly in front of me.

"Um, I think your poem was incredibly beautiful. Whoever you were talking about up there is a lucky woman," she said.

"Yeah, she can be a lucky woman," I said as soon as her fiancé walked up.

"Hey, honey, are you ready to go?" he asked as he kissed her on the lips.

Then he looked at me.

"Hello. I'm Derrick Kennedi's fiancé. Are you one of her coworkers?" he asked.

"No, he is the guy who helped me out when I had car problems and was stranded on the side of the road," Kennedi said.

"Oh, wow! Let me give you a few dollars for helping out my girl," Thomas said as he started to reach into his wallet.

"No, thank you, my man. I already got my reward," I said, looking right into Kennedi's eyes.

"You guys have a good night," I said as I walked off, feeling eyes on the back of my head as I left.

CHAPTER 13
Kennedi

"Hello, mother," I said as I walked into my office on another Monday after an awfully long weekend.

After Julian made his comment last night, Derrick and I have been going through it ever since.

"Don't 'hello, Mother' me. You have now been engaged for three months, and you still have not picked out a wedding date. I believe you guys should get married this year, if I do say so myself," she said.

"Mother, can we talk about this later after I get off work?" I said.

"Don't be foolish and let a good man like Derrick go. He was a lot better than your no-good daddy," she said.

She kept going on and on about Derrick, saying that *Derrick is an excellent provider; you would never have to work a day in your life; you may even have to quit your job so you can take care of the kids,* blah-blah-blah.

"Listen, Mom. Gabriella just walked in. I have to go."

I finally ushered my mom off the phone.

"Ms. Toni is back at it again, I see," Gabriella said, taking a seat across from me and glowing.

Come to think of it, I have not spoken to Gabriella the whole weekend. The only time I saw her was when we all met at the jazz club.

"What is going on with you? There is a certain glow that you have, and I'm loving it."

Gabriella looked at me and tried to hide her blushing.

"Well, do you remember the guy Thomas I was telling you about and whom you have met a few times? Well, since we reconnected at the grocery store, we have been talking nonstop," Gabriella said.

"Well, I am really happy for you guys," I said, genuinely happy that my best friend has found someone that she really likes and treats her with respect.

"Thanks, I actually came in here to ask you for a favor. Thomas and Julian are looking to get a place for their trucking business, and since you know about land and property, I figured I should give Julian your work number. He will be calling you shortly to go over some details," Gabriella said.

"Cool! I could always use some more business."

That is what I said on the outside, but on the inside, I felt like a nervous wreck being pulled into this situation of having to show a man around, who I am extremely attracted to. If I were not engaged, he would be the type of guy I would like to get to know, but he probably has a girlfriend already, which should not matter to me anyway.

"Great, so he should be giving you a call a little later on in the day," Gabriella said as she got up to walk out of the office.

After she left, I continued with the rest of my day, and then I got a phone call.

"Hello," I said.

"Hello, is this Kennedi?" I heard the familiar voice say.

"Yes, this is Kennedi," I said.

"Hello. Gabriella told me to call you today about looking at new properties for my business," he said in his smooth, silky voice.

"Yes, would you be available tomorrow to look at some properties, and if you find something you like, you can talk it over with your partner, and we can start some paperwork made up for you to get the ball rolling," I said.

"Yeah, that would be great with me. Can we make it around 2:00 p.m. tomorrow?" He said, and that was when I heard a bit of his country twang.

"Yeah, that would be good for me. You have a good rest of your day, Julian," I said.

"I hope the rest of your day is just as beautiful as you are, Kennedi," he said right before he hung up.

CHAPTER 14
Julian

"So, as you can see, this building has the features you would need. It has two large office spaces, perfect for you and your business partners."

I heard Kennedi go on and on about the place, but all I could focus on was the sway in her hips and how the midi skirt she was wearing was making a peekaboo of her smooth thigh.

"So, what do you think?" she turned around and asked me, breaking me out of my lustful stare.

"I like it. The property looks good, and I already took a few pictures of the place and sent them to Thomas. He is on board with it," I said.

Then she looked at me in the face and asked, "Where are you from?"

"I'm from South Carolina, but I moved up here to Michigan when both of my parents died in a car crash. But I guess I still have that little southern twang with me. What about you?" I asked as I leaned against the wall behind me, and she was standing right in front of me with her arms and legs crossed.

"I am a proud Michigan girl through and through. I went to college at the University of Michigan, where I got my undergrad and grad degrees in law, and I decided to focus on contract law dealing with business, land, and different buildings, and I have a knack for the small print," she said.

"That's not all you have a knack for. I heard you singing. You have a beautiful voice. You should definitely come to the jazz club and sing. Your voice is beautiful," I said.

"Well, you know, when I was in high school, I had plans on becoming a professional singer, but my mom was like, 'That is not a real career,' so that was how law came into play," she said.

"Wow! That is amazing! But I don't think you should sleep on a voice like yours, even if it is just at open-mic nights," I said.

"Yeah, maybe me and my fiancée will come to the next open-mic night," she said with her back turned to me.

"Can I ask you a personal question?" I said.

"Sure," she said with her back still facing me.

"How did you know that your fiancée was the one for you?" I said.

"Well, I really didn't know, but we both worked in the same building, and one day we were on the same elevator, and he asked me out. We started dating, and the rest is history," she said.

"Have you guys set a wedding date yet?" I said.

"No, umm, not really," she said.

"Looking at you and just spending a few moments with you, I can tell he is a very lucky man to get a woman like you," I said as I walked up closer to her from behind.

"Yeah, umm, we are both very lucky," she said as she turned around, ran right into my chest, and looked up at me straight in the eyes.

"Are you really in love with him?" I said as I stood planted with my hands on each side of her, locking her in so she couldn't move.

"Yes, I'm in love with him. Why do you ask that question?" she said.

"Because if you were truly in love with him, you would not have been thinking about me since the day that we met. Look me straight in the eyes and say that you have not," I said.

She looked at me and opened her mouth, but nothing came out of it. Her chest was heaving up and down.

"Do you want to kiss me right now?" I asked her.

She just shook her head up and down, and I did something about it from the first moment I saw her. I pulled her body closer to mine and tilted her head back. I pressed my mouth against her soft lips, and it started slowly, and then it got more intense. Just when I was about to pull away, she moaned in my mouth, and that caused my dick to become more bricked as I grabbed her ass and pulled her closer so she could feel how hard my dick was.

"Julian, what are we about to do?" she moaned in my mouth.

"Something that we both wanted to do since the very first moment we saw each other. If you want me to stop, you better tell me now," I said.

"No, I don't want you to stop," she said as she began to unbutton my pants and put her small hands in my boxers as she started to stroke my already hard dick.

I did not know it could get any harder when she said, "I want to suck your dick."

"No," I said, "I want to taste you first."

I picked her up and laid her on the desk in the office. I pushed her skirt up and rubbed on her clit through her panties, and I could see how wet she really was.

"Why are you so wet?"

I did not even give her a good chance to respond before my tongue was already tasting her sweetness.

"Oh, shit! Julian, you are going to make me cum like that," she said.

"Can you cum all over my tongue? I want to taste all your sweet juices," I said.

Just when she was about to cum, I came up. I didn't know if she wanted me to kiss her or not, but when she said, "Kiss me," then it was all over from there. I guided my dick into her wetness, and that was all she wrote.

CHAPTER 15
Kennedi

When did this bed become so hard? I thought to myself as I opened my eyes, and I was in an unfamiliar place. Then I noticed that I was not by myself when I felt a strange arm that was not my fiancé's.

"Good morning."

I heard a male voice next to me, and then it all came back—what had happened between me and Julian the day before and how we ended up where we are. I shot off the desk.

"I have to go. This was a terrible mistake," I said.

"What was so terrible about it?" Julian asked.

"I have a fiancée, and I am not a cheater," I said as I got up off the desk and started to put my clothes on piece by piece.

"Why do you keep rejecting what you want? It's obvious that it's not your fiancée that you want," he said as he looked at me.

I tried to ignore his stare.

"Me and my fiancée go through our ups and downs like any other couple, but—"

"Look me in the eyes and tell me that you don't feel a connection between us," he said.

"I have to go. I don't have time to deal with this right now," I said.

I left him out there, and I hurried home. When I pulled into my driveway, I noticed that Derrick was sitting in his car. He got out of his car when he saw me pulling up into the driveway.

"I have been calling you all night. Where have you been?" he asked.

"I was over Gabriella's house, but she had to go over her boyfriend's house, so she just left me at her house. I had a little bit too much to drink and woke up late. So, all I need to do is get ready for work," I said as I started walking into my house.

"I came by here to follow up on our wedding date because we cannot keep skating around the fact that we are getting married very soon. I spoke to your mom about the wedding, and we both agreed that it should be before this year is out," Derrick said.

"You know what? I don't have time to discuss this right now. I will see you at work," I said.

I grabbed my phone and texted Gabriella what I just told Derrick, just in case he decided to go and talk to her. Then I got in the shower and pretended not to be affected by what I just did—cheating on my fiancé and still trying to convince myself that I do not feel anything for Julian.

CHAPTER 16
Julian

"Pass the ball, man," I said to Thomas.

On Thursday, we get together to play basketball at our local gym, and the way my week has been going, I desperately needed to get together with my ninjas to shoot around a little.

"That's game," I said as I made the shot to put us up when there was only a little bit of time left remaining on the shot clock.

After I finished dapping everyone up, I went to sit on the bench where Thomas was already sitting, talking on the phone, and grinning like a damn Cheshire cat.

"Who are you talking on the phone with?" I said while trying to grab his phone.

"Man, go on. I'm talking to Gabriella," Thomas said.

"Whipped ass," I said as Thomas was starting to get off the phone.

"Who the fuck are you talking to like that?" Thomas said as he stood up aggressively.

"I'm talking to you," I said as I stood up to look him in the eyes.

We both had a face-off for about one minute, then we both busted out laughing.

"Man, I am not about to even face you. I am really feeling Gabriella. I'm glad I found her after all these years after high school," Thomas said.

"Well, even though I don't really believe in all this love shit, I'm glad that you found someone that you vibe with on a deep level," I said.

"Man, you say that shit now, but wait until you finally meet HER," Thomas said.

"But how was the meeting with Kennedi earlier this week? I didn't get a chance to ask you about it earlier," Thomas said.

"Umm, yeah, the meeting went good. We found a good place that would be good for our trucking company. There were two offices and enough space for us to start out with our four trucks."

"You fucked her, didn't you?" Thomas said while he looked at me with an accusatory glare.

"No, I didn't—"

"Don't fix your face to lie to me. It's written all over your face," Thomas cut in before I was able to finish my sentence.

"Okay, I slept with her, but it was a mistake that will never happen again," I said.

"Man, that is Gabriella's best friend, and not to mention that she is engaged. We don't need that drama in our life right now," Thomas said.

I knew Thomas was right when he said that we didn't need drama, but I could not help but think that this is only the beginning of a very long road between Kennedi and me.

CHAPTER 17

Kennedi

"Bitch, what are you not telling me? And why are you telling me to lie if Derrick asked me where you were last night?" Gabriella asked as she burst into my office in her fashionable way, of course.

"What are you talking about? And can you please keep your voice down?" I said as I got up and made sure that my door was locked before we had an uninvited guest.

"Don't act surprised. Why would you need me to lie about your whereabouts to your fiancé?" Gabriella asked as she looked at me with a suspicious glare.

"I, um, made a mistake last night—I accidently slept with Julian," I said in a hushed tone while I laid my head down on the desk.

"Kennedi, really? Well, how was it?" Gabriella asked in an exciting voice.

"Really? I just told you I slept with another man who is not my fiancé, and you are asking me how the sex was," I said in disbelief.

"Well, yeah, I want to know how the sex was. But in all honesty, how do you feel about cheating on your fiancé, whom you don't really love, with a man whom you obviously have not stopped thinking about since the first time you met?" Gabriella said in complete disbelief.

"Okay, fine. I enjoyed the sex, but I know that it is nothing. Anyway, Julian seems like a player. He has all the ladies throwing their panties at him when we went to jazz club, and even if I was interested, it would not work because he is a bit too young and still trying to get his shit together," I said.

"I understand what you are saying. But from what I could see at the club, he was only checking you even when your fiancé showed up. Ohh, and I forgot to ask the most important question—where, when, and how did this happen?" Gabriella asked.

"Well, it was when I was showing him a certain property that our firm is affiliated with. We started talking, and before I knew it, we were in one of the offices, face down, ass up with Julian behind me," I said in disbelief.

"In a commercial property, girllll! I hope that there were no cameras in there," Gabriella said.

I laid my head back on the desk and wondered what else would happen to me today.

CHAPTER 18

Julian

"Man, why the fuck are you bringing me here as a third wheel? I don't want to see you and Gabriella slob all over each other," I said as Thomas was dragging me inside the new restaurant called 7even.

"Man, I told you. Gabriella was bringing a friend for you to meet," Thomas said as we walked into the new restaurant.

"Reservations under the name Thomas."

As we were about to follow the hostess to be seated, I noticed Gabriella walking in with Kennedi. My eyes could not believe what I was seeing. When Thomas said Gabriella was bringing a friend for me, I did not expect to see Kennedi again. We locked eyes for a moment, and it seemed like everyone else in the room disappeared. I had to hurry and look away before I got too caught up. *What the fuck is*

51

wrong with me? I noticed Kennedi looking as shocked and surprised as I was when she and Gabriella finally made their way over to where we were. I could smell her scent.

"Hey, baby," I heard Thomas say to Gabriella while they embraced in an intimate hug.

When Kennedi finally looked at me, she softly said, "Hi," with a slight smile.

"Hey," I said.

"It looks like we were bombarded into their lovely relationship," Kennedi said once she reached me.

Before I had a chance to respond, Thomas yelled, "Our table is over here."

We were all the way in the back booth. Gabriella and Thomas decided to sit next to each other, so that required me to sit next to Kennedi. It was hard work for me to keep my hands to myself.

"If you all could excuse me for one moment, I have to head to the gentleman's room," Thomas said.

Not even a minute later, Gabriella got up and excused herself. Then the waiter came to the table, and I just ordered a round of drinks for everyone. Once the waiter left, silence came over the table. I didn't necessarily know how to start a conversation, so I just said the first thing that came to mind.

"How is the wedding planning going?" I asked, knowing I didn't give a damn.

"Umm, it's going well. Our families are pretty excited for our union," Kennedi said.

I guess my being quiet gave her the green light to keep going.

"Does he know that we fucked?" I said in a less-than-pleasant tone.

"Why are you doing this right now?" she asked through clinched teeth.

"I just thought I would ask. While you are so enamored with wedding planning, I think you miss telling your fiancé the most important thing," I said with a shrug.

"You know what?" Kennedi couldn't finish her statement because Thomas and Gabriella were walking toward us, looking all disheveled.

"I know you two were not fucking in the bathroom," I said, and then the two looked at each other like they just got caught, and then we all busted out laughing.

CHAPTER 19
Kennedi

Today is the day I go in for the final fitting of my wedding dress. When I arrived at Upscale Wedding Boutique, I saw that my mother was there with my future mother-in-law, sitting down and having a drink of champagne. I also invited Gabriella to come, but I haven't seen her yet. Maybe she is just running a little late.

"Hello, Mother," I said, walking in.

"Oн, here she comes—the bride to be," my mother said when she stood up to greet me.

"Hello, darling," my mother-in-law said.

Both my mother and mother-in-law are in their sixties, but you would never know by looking at them. My mother was dressed in leather pants and a one-shoulder black bodysuit, and her hair was cut in a short pixie cut. While my future mother-in-law was dressed in a sweater dress and black pumps.

"Well, now that the bride has joined us, are we waiting for anyone else?" the saleslady asked.

"Ummm, I was expecting my friend to come, but we can go ahead and start putting on my dress," I said.

"Alright, dear. Let's get ready to make you the talk of the country," the saleslady said as we headed back to the dressing room.

When I came out of the dressing room, I heard my mom and mother-in-law gasp.

"Wowww! You look absolutely gorgeous!"

"You are going to be a beautiful bride!"

Those are some of the statements I heard from the wedding dress staff and everyone in between. After the wedding dress fitting, I was expecting to hear something from Gabriela by this time. Not that it was going on at 10:00 p.m. After the fitting, I went to visit Derrick in his office.

"Hey, babe," he said as I opened the door to his office.

"What brings you to this side of town?" he asked.

"I told you last night that I had a final dress fitting downtown today."

While I still haven't told him about me sleeping with Julian, I figured it wouldn't matter that much, especially since it was a one-time mistake and would never happen again.

"Ohhhhh, yeah. I remember you telling me about that. How did it go?" he asked as he got up out of his chair and came to greet me in an embrace.

"It went well. The dress fitted beautifully," I said.

"I am sure you are going to be the most beautiful bride in the world, and we are going to be the perfect couple. I will continue to rise to the top as one of the best lawyers, and you, my beautiful wife, will be able to quit your job and become a stay-at-home wife to our four beautiful children," he said.

"Derrick, I didn't say anything about quitting my job. Furthermore, we never discussed what type of household we would have when we decided to have children," I said.

"Well, Kennedi, I thought that was what we both wanted—for you to stay home and raise the kids," he said.

"I do want to raise my children, but—"

"Babe, can you hold on for a second?"

The ringing of my phone brought me out of my trance.

"Girl, where have you been?" I said to Gabriella as I answered the phone.

"We have been at the hospital all day. Julian's grandmother just passed away," she said in a hushed tone.

"Ohhhhh, my goodness! What hospital are you guys at?" I said while rushing to throw some clothes on.

"Bresham Hospital."

"I am on my way."

CHAPTER 20

Julian

Today started like any other normal day. Before I went to work, I would go and check on my grandmother, but this morning felt different. Usually, when I walked into her house, I was greeted with the smell of coffee brewing. But all the lights were off, and she didn't answer when I called her by her usual name, G-ma.

"G-ma, what are you still doing in bed?"

When I got closer to her bed, I noticed that something was not right. That's when I called 911. They rushed her to the hospital. They did try to resuscitate her, but it was no good. My favorite girl was gone, and there was nothing I could do about it.

"We should get you home, man," Thomas said while my eyes were still glued to the floor, tears threatening my eyes.

"Julian." I heard someone say my name, and the last person I expected to see was Kennedi heading my way.

"I am so sorry for your loss," she said as she sat down beside me and pulled me into a tight embrace.

I could no longer contain my tears. I just let them flow as she consoled me. The drive back home was one that was very quiet and daunting because I was not looking forward to driving past G-ma's house on the way home. Even though it was midnight, I have programmed her front porch light to turn on when it reaches 8:00 p.m. As the three of us got out of Thomas's car, Kennedi stepped out of her car since she had followed us. We all got out of the car to walk into my place. I couldn't help but realize that my life would never be the same.

"Alright, man. I guess we will get going," Thomas said as he and Gabriella got up after being here for over an hour.

"Kennedi, do you want us to walk you to your car?" Thomas asked as he and Gabriella were about to leave.

"No, I think I am going to stay for a little while longer," Kennedi said.

"Well, alright. I will talk to you guys later. I'll check in with you soon," Thomas said as he and Gabriella were walking out of the house.

"You didn't have to stay here," I said, and that caused her to turn around and look at me.

"I know. I wanted to make sure you were okay," she said while looking around my place.

"Won't your husband wonder where you are at this time of the night?" I said.

"First off, he is not my husband yet. Why do you keep bringing him up? Are you jealous?" she said.

"Why the fuck would I be jealous?" I said.

"Because I am getting married, and you have a different woman Monday–Friday."

"I would rather be single than about to marry someone I don't love."

"I love my fiancé. Furthermore, I—"

"Then why did you fuck me?" I said, interrupting her statement.

"That was a mistake, and obviously, me staying here is a mistake. So I will just get my shit and leave," she said, grabbing her bag and keys.

"Ohh, shit! I didn't know Ms. Proper had that language in you," I said, getting up from the couch.

"You don't know me, Julian," she said, heading toward the front door.

"I know you don't love your fiancé," I said, which made her stop in her tracks.

"I know you want to see if there is something better for you. You want to see if I am better for you, but you are scared. Why are you scared?" I asked, standing right behind her.

"I am not scared of you, Julian," she said, turning around.

"I am scared of hurting the people I love the most, and I—"

"Tell me you don't want me, and I will let you walk out. I will not bother you anymore, but you have to tell me that you don't want me," I said as I started to pull her body closer to mine.

"What about my—" she was saying before I put my lips on hers, and the way she kissed me back told me everything I needed to know.

CHAPTER 21

Kennedi

I was not expecting to end this night with Julian's tongue in my mouth, or maybe I did.

"Julian, take me to the bedroom," I said breathlessly.

"I will, sweetheart, but I want to make memories of you and your sexy body in every area of my house, starting in my living room," he said as he left me standing by the door and went to sit on the couch.

"Strip for me," he said so authoritatively that it made my nipples hard and my pussy pulsating.

I started to take my shirt off and started to tease him when I started playing with my nipples through my lace bra.

"Take off your pants now," Julian said, making me look at him.

I started to walk over to him and stood right in front of him while I took my pants off, and he started kissing my stomach slowly. He moved my hands and started taking my panties off for me. He stuck to his word about having me in every area of his house.

"Good morning," I heard Julian say, which woke me up along with the smell of freshly brewed coffee and breakfast consisting of waffles, bacon, an omelet, and sausage.

"What is all this?" I asked.

"I just thought you would need your energy after last night," he said, looking like Adonis with his dreads hanging low, his shirt off, and gray sweatpants. I could tell that he didn't have any boxers on.

"I appreciate that. It looks delicious and tastes even better," I said, eyeing him up and down.

"Don't you look at me like that, or you will end up becoming my breakfast," he said while getting in bed with me.

I started to eat my breakfast in silence with all these thoughts rushing through my head: *What have I done? Do I break off my engagement? What will I tell my mom? What would people think of my decision to be with Julian? What will my colleagues say?*

"Are you okay?" Julian asked, looking at me with concern in his eyes.

"Yeah, I am okay. Just thinking," I said.

"Are you thinking about how you are going to break it off with your fiancé?" Julian asked.

"Don't you think that is moving a little fast? Considering we have not talked about being in a relationship with each other, and you want me to go and just say goodbye to a three-year relationship," I said, frantically looking for my clothes as I try to find a way to escape.

"I don't share my woman. So either you want to be with me and only me fully, or we can end this thing right here," Julian said in a matter-of-fact tone.

"Wait, babe. Let's not argue. I don't like to share either, so that means you will have to tell all your little girlfriends that you will no longer be available," I said as we started to get comfortable together on bed.

"You don't have to worry about any other woman. In this short amount of time, you have shown me what love could be and how beautiful it could be when you experience it with the right person," Julian said, rubbing his fingers through my short hair.

"Julian, I can't promise you anything, but I can say that I have not felt this way for anyone, not even for my fiancé. It gives my heart that extra flutter that you give me, and I promise that I am committed to seeing where things could go with you. I am no longer going to be scared about anything anymore, including being with you," I said, knowing my life will never be the same as it once was when I tell the news to everyone. I just hope everyone can live with my decision, including me.

CHAPTER 22
Julian

The night that my grandmother died had to be one of the most unbelievable yet saddest nights of my life. I lost my favorite girl, but then came another love that I was not expecting. It has been two months since we have been in an official relationship. I have started driving more trucks, and my business is growing tremendously. *Yeah, a nigga used the word tremendously.* I have a fine-assed woman by my side who I seem to be falling in love with more each day. Right now, I am about to grab her favorite coffee and take it to her office to surprise her. I was in the elevator heading toward her floor when I got in sight of Gabriella. Her eyes went frantically from me to Kennedi's door, which was shut.

"Hey, Gabriella, is Kennedi in a meeting?" I asked her, not wanting the coffee to get cold.

"Umm, hey, Julian. No, she is not in a meeting right now, but I think she is a bit preoccupied," Gabriella said in a bit of a panic.

As I was heading toward her door, I heard her voice becoming louder the more she talked to whoever she was talking to. The more I listened, the more I realized that I needed to march my ass on in there.

"Do we have a problem?" I said as I opened her door, and I saw her ex-fiancé standing a little too close to her face, saying stupid shit.

As soon as I said that, both of them turned to look at me, and then Kennedi said, "Babe, what are you doing here?" She walked toward me in her gray pantsuit that held her curves in all the right places, and it took all of me not to drool just by looking at her.

"I thought you might need this after last night," I said as she blushed.

I looked over to see Derrick's face getting so fucking red, and that brought a satisfied smile to my face.

"I think the business you have in here is over," I said.

"You can't tell me to leave," his punk ass said.

"You can either get the fuck out, or I will throw you the fuck out," I said, heading toward him, and then Kennedi came in the middle of us.

"Derrick, can you please leave? You are no longer wanted here, EVER!" Kennedi stated in a matter-of-fact tone.

"This isn't over. You haven't seen the last of me," Derrick said with a smirk on his face.

"Yeah, that's what I thought. I bet you haven't even met her mom yet," he said as he was walking out.

I started to go after him, but Kennedi pulled my arm.

"He is not even worth it, babe."

Kennedi put her arms around my waist.

"Do you love me?" I asked, looking into her eyes.

"Of course I love you. Why do you ask me that?" Kennedi said.

"We have been dating for the past two months, and you haven't introduced me to your mother yet," I said as we started to untwine from each other, and she started to walk back to her desk chair.

"You know I have been really busy with work, babe, and I haven't had the time to really talk to her about anything," she said.

"It seems like you guys talk every other day, and you have brought up my name once," I said in a questioning tone.

"Babe, once the timing is right, I will tell her. Thanks again for the coffee," she said as she went back to her desk.

I could be wrong, but something told me that there is much more to this story that I am not going to like. I just hope that I am wrong about my gut feeling.

CHAPTER 23
Kennedi

It was a surprise when Derrick came into my office this morning, even though we work in the same building. For the past two months, I have been able to avoid him since breaking off our engagement.

"Spill the tea. I've got twenty minutes to spare," Gabriella said as she barged into my office.

"There is no tea to spill. I didn't know that Derrick was planning on coming to my office this morning, and I was not expecting to get such a sweet, unexpected visit from Julian," I said.

"Girllll! I thought it was about to be a throw-down between Julian and Derrick," Gab said with a chuckle.

"But seriously, Kennedi, why haven't you told your mother about Julian yet? I have seen you talk to

your mother multiple times, and you don't say anything about Julian."

"Gab, girl, relax. It is cool. I'm cool. Julian is
cool," I said as I went back to typing.

"Julian is a good man, and if you can't see that
now, then it would probably be best if you left him
alone before anyone gets hurt," Gab said.

"I love Julian, and I see a future for us. Trust and
believe that I know exactly what I am doing."

CHAPTER 24
Julian

While I was doing my regular truck rounds that took me to Kennedi's side of town, I thought about going by her place to bring her some breakfast, until I spotted her having breakfast with a woman I instantly recognized.

"Hi, sexy. I thought I recognized you over here."

When I said that I could leave her body when I walked over there, "Hey, Julian, what are you doing over on this side of town?" Kennedi asked, looking nervously between me and the woman I believe to be her mother.

"I had to do a job on this side of town. I just came in here to grab some breakfast, and then I will be getting back on the road," I said.

"Who is this, Kennedi?" her mother asked with her eyebrow raised.

"Umm, well, Mom, this is my friend Julian."

"Is that all I am to you?" I asked, looking her right in the eyes.

"Julian, can we talk about this outside?" Kennedi asked with pleading eyes.

"There is nothing for us to talk about. Take care of yourself, Kennedi," I said while walking out.

I heard her trying to get my attention, but I kept walking. In that moment, I knew it was best for me to let go of the situation and finally let go of Kennedi as I walked out of the restaurant.

CHAPTER 25
Kennedi

I did not think I would run into Julian this morning, and I did not plan on him storming out of the restaurant the way he did.

"Well, that young man is certainly handsome, but he is not the man you need in your life," my mother said as I came and sat back down.

"What type of man do I need in my life, mother? A man like Derrick?" I asked.

"You watch your tone with me, young lady," she said.

"I apologize, but if you think I am going back to Derrick, you can give that up. He was a self-centered, egotistical man who was more in love with himself than me. So, when I met Julian, he showed me what true, unselfish love looks like," I said.

"If that is true, my dear, then why didn't you introduce me to him? When I first met your father, I didn't hide him, and I definitely didn't introduce him as just my friend to my mother. So, obviously you don't like him as much as you thought you did to just introduce him as just your friend. I could tell by the look in his eyes that he loves you, and you have shown that you do not have the same love for him. You need to leave him alone and don't play with his emotions," my mother said.

As soon as my mother stopped talking, the waitress came up to the table, and that stopped me from saying what I was going to say, and to be honest, I didn't have any rebuttal to what she just said.

CHAPTER 26
Julian

Knock, knock.

"Thomas, are you home?"

It was now 7:00 p.m., and I tried calling him, but he would not answer the phone.

"Julian, what is going on, man?" Thomas said.

"Sorry if I am interrupting things," I said when I saw Gabriella in the kitchen.

"Gaby, can you tell your friend to stop calling me? Tell her it is over."

"When did you guys break up?" Gaby asked.

"It's a long story, Gab. I am sorry for the interruption, but I just really need to talk to Thomas right now," I said.

"No problem," Gab said as she headed back to the bedroom.

When I finished telling Thomas what happened, his face was in shock.

"Wow, man! I was hoping that she was the one for you. I enjoyed seeing you all happy and shit. Now it is going to be awkward at the wedding," Thomas said slyly.

"What? Man, congratulations, man!" I said, standing up and giving him a hug.

"Damn, you are about to become somebody's husband," I said in disbelief.

"You know I want you to be my best man," Thomas said.

"Of course, man, whatever you need," I said.

I couldn't be happier for my brother from another mother, but I couldn't help but feel some jealousy, wondering if my time would ever come.

CHAPTER 27
Kennedi

Please, pick up. Please, pick up.

I have been calling Julian for the past hour, and he has yet to pick up. I did not know that my day was going to go the way it did. I was supposed to have breakfast with my mother, and then later in the day I was supposed to have cuddles with my boo. When I heard my phone ring, I got excited.

"Hello," I said anxiously.

"What did I tell you, Kennedi?"

That was when I noticed that it was Gaby on the other end.

"I didn't mean to let today happen," I said.

"But you did, Kennedi, and now Julian is over here talking to my fiancé about what you did."

She caught me off guard when she said fiancé.

"What did you say, Gabriella? You said you have a whattt!" I asked excitedly.

"Yes, Thomas asked me to marry him tonight, and I said yes," Gabriella said excitedly.

"I am soooo happy for you guys!" I said, genuinely excited for my friend.

"But back to you, Kennedi. What happened?" Gab asked.

"Well, I was at breakfast with my mother, and I was caught off guard when Julian came up. I wasn't quite ready to introduce him to my mother, so I just introduced him as my friend," I said.

"Kennedi, you have really hurt Julian. I don't think you can come back from this, but I just don't want it to be awkward at my wedding," Gab said.

"Don't worry, Julian just needs some time to cool down, and we will come back like we never left. You'll see."

ONE YEAR LATER

"You look absolutely stunning, Gaby."

Today is the day my best friend gets married.

"Awww, don't make me cry," Gaby said, fanning her face and trying not to ruin her makeup.

"How are you feeling about seeing Julian again?" Gaby asked.

Things between Julian and I did not go as expected. He never returned any of my phone calls, and I have not run into him anywhere around town.

"Ohhhhh, girl, please, I feel fine. I moved on. *Not really, but I am not going to admit that out loud.* I am pretty sure that he has moved on, so it was fun while it lasted," I said, trying to convince myself.

"Yeah, I heard him tell Thomas he planned on bringing a date," Gaby said.

"Well, good for him, but enough about me. Let's go get you marriedddd!"

JULIAN

I knew Kennedi was going to be here, and I was not looking forward to it. I haven't seen or spoken to her since that morning, when I saw her having breakfast with her mother. I thought about that day constantly, and one thing I will never let happen is a woman making me feel like I am not good enough for her.

"Are you alright, my boy?" Thomas said as he came to the bar I was at.

"Yeah, I am…"

I got distracted because I saw Kennedi walking up to the bar, looking sexy as hell. It looked like she got thicker. The dress she was wearing looked scrumptious on her body. *I would have loved to take a bite.* And the way her hair was, I could even see that smile, *damn.*

"Congratulations, my brother. Make sure you take care of my girl," Kennedi said while giving Thomas a hug.

"No doubt about that, sis. I am about to go find my wife. I'll catch up with you guys later," Thomas said.

I was about to walk off.

"How are you doing, Julian?" I heard Kennedi ask, and that made me stop right in my tracks.

"Doing good," I said dryly.

She started to walk closer to me, where I could smell her sweet perfume.

"Would you like to dance?" she asked.

"Nahhh, I'm good," I said, and I tried walking off again.

"Julian, please," she said.

I took a deep breath.

"Lead the way," I said.

While she was walking in front of me, it took everything in me not to stare at her plump assets.

"It is really good to see you again, Julian. I feel like I owe you an explanation."

"Kennedi, that was over a year ago. No need for an explanation," I said while trying to maintain my hand on her waist.

"But I want to, Julian. I was more concerned about what my mother would say about me dating you than the feeling that I get when I am with you."

She paused for a second to see if I would interrupt her.

"Julian, you have shown me the most amazing love in three months than I have had in years with my prior relationship. You definitely were not just a friend to me. You were my lover, best friend, and confidant. I am so sorry if I made you feel like you were not good enough for me. I can understand if you never want to see me after this. I understand," she said while walking away.

"I will not tolerate being hidden from anyone."

That stopped her a little bit. She looked at me and then at the front of the reception, where Gabby and Thomas were sitting.

"Hold on," she said.

I had no idea what she was about to do until I heard, "Umm, hello, hello, can everyone hear me?" Kennedi asked in her microphone.

She was standing on a chair.

"I just wanted to say that I am deeply in love with Julian Knight."

I started toward where she was. And I could see the people at the reception looking a little confused.

"You are the man I want, and I would like the whole world to know how much you mean to me. I hope that you will have me," she said as I helped her down off the chair.

"You are the craziest, most spontaneous, and sexiest woman I have ever met, and I am so glad it was you I met that fateful night. I love you, Kennedi, and I will have you for a lifetime and then some."

The End

ABOUT THE AUTHOR

Epiphany A. Hightower is twenty-six years old and from Georgia. She loves to read and has a passion for all things black love. She discovered her passion for writing while she was in college. Music, fashion, traveling, watching films, reading, and writing are some things she likes to do during her free time. You can follow her on Instagram at epiphany_anette.

www.ingramcontent.com/pod-product-compliance
Lightning Source LLC
Chambersburg PA
CBHW022049150726
47990CB00003B/1024